TO FIND THE WAY

TO FIND THE WAY

Susan Nunes   Illustrated by Cissy Gray

UNIVERSITY OF HAWAII PRESS
•
CURRICULUM RESEARCH & DEVELOPMENT GROUP
UNIVERSITY OF HAWAII

92 93 94 95 96 97 5 4 3 2 1

Library of Congress Cataloging-in-Publication Data
Nunes, Susan, 1943–
To find the way / Susan Nunes; illustrated by Cissy Gray.
p. cm. — (A Kolowalu book)
Summary: Using his knowledge of the sea and stars, Vahi-roa the navigator guides a group of Tahitians aboard a great canoe to the unknown islands of Hawaii.
ISBN 0–8248–1376–6
[1. Hawaii—Fiction. 2. Voyages and travels—Fiction. 3. Sea stories.]
I. Gray, Cissy, ill. II. Title.
PZ7.N96454Se 1992
[Fic]—dc 20 91-31334

Printed in Singapore

Calligraphy by John Prestianni
Designed by Barbara Pope

For the navigators

Now is the season for sailing,
Blow, blow, gods of the wind.
Wake the right wind,
A straight wind,
Take us from Tahiti
On the sea path north,
To a horizon never crossed,
To an island far away.

At last! The time for sailing had come. Weather, wind, stars—all the signs were right. Long months of preparation were over. Ceremonies and farewells were done. Now the great canoe could set off to sea. The men and women lining the decks looked shoreward for a last glimpse of loved ones. Their destination was islands far to the north where no one in memory had sailed before. This was a voyage of settlement, and those chosen to go were leaving Tahiti forever.

Standing at the stern of the canoe, Teva strained to find his mother among the people on shore, but she was lost to him. "Goodbye!" he called out, hoping she would hear him. "Goodbye! Goodbye!" Through his tears, he watched his village and valley drift away.

Someone put a comforting hand on Teva's shoulder. It was the navigator, Vahi-roa. Priest and high chief, Vahi-roa possessed the knowledge to find the way.

Teva looked up at the old man and smiled bravely. "I'm all right, Grandfather," he said.

"It takes courage to say goodbye," said Vahi-roa. "Your father would be proud."

The year before, Teva's father had been lost in a great storm, and ever since, Teva had sailed with Vahi-roa. The boy took a deep breath and drew strength from the memory of his father. Though only a child, he, Teva, had been chosen to sail.

Vahi-roa returned to his place on the navigator's platform and signaled to the steersman to change course. Now the wind blew across the decks and filled the sails. The great canoe came to life. Teva felt its power.

And what power! For this was a voyaging canoe built to sail long distances over the deep sea. At launching, the priests had named her *Ari'i-ati-tai,* Princess-Surrounded-by-the-Sea, and had given her to this journey. Beneath Teva's feet the platform felt solid and strong. He looked up at the sails, at the feathered pennants streaming in the wind. What an honor to sail, he thought.

As the sun set into the sea, Vahi-roa studied the long waves and the surge of water past the hulls. He motioned to the steersman to align the stern of the canoe with the island they were leaving behind.

Teva watched his homeland grow smaller. "Tahiti, still in my sight!" he called. While the light lasted, he looked back as if to fix forever the place on the horizon where his home island lay.

The stars appeared. The Cluster-of-Four edged over the horizon. Soon it would climb high into the sky behind them. The voyagers' home star, Festivity-of-Chiefs, would pass straight overhead.

Teva pointed to the guide stars rising one by one in the east. "Look, Grandfather. Our old friends." He called each one by name.

Vahi-roa nodded. "By their path we have steered in our home waters. Soon we must look for new friends."

Teva welcomed the familiar stars and wondered what names his new friends would have. His grandfather's sky was larger than the boy could imagine.

When it was time to rest, Teva curled up beside the crowded sleeping hut. For a long time he watched the stars overhead. He thought about his mother, about friends left behind. What lay ahead? He looked at the familiar shape of his grandfather. Vahi-roa stood on the platform with the steersman. Their voices comforted the boy and he slept.

The sky was still dark when Teva awoke. His grandfather gazed at the heavens. Soon Vahi-roa would use the rising sun and fading stars to adjust his course. Teva knew how important mornings were. He watched his grandfather read the signs.

In the east the sky began to glow. Clouds moved high above the horizon. A brisk wind filled the sails. Good weather, thought Teva. He looked for the canoe's counting rope. Vahi-roa had tied a single knot to mark their first night at sea.

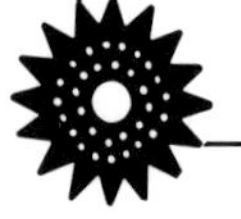

Teva quickly ate his morning meal of fish and sweet potato. He could smell the smoke from the cooking fire. Two men held the center steering paddle. Nearby a woman stood watch. Others baited the fishing lines, fed the caged animals, and aired damp bedding. Everyone shared the work. Only wayfinding was Vahi-roa's alone.

When it was his turn to bail, Teva slid into one of the hulls and joined others busy at this endless task. Water continuously seeped in or washed over the hulls. Before long, Teva was drenched with sweat and salt water. He could hear pigs grunting and chickens squawking in the cages above him. Coconuts stored in the hull now bobbed around his knees. Teva concentrated on lifting the heavy scoop. He looked forward to joining his grandfather on the navigator's platform.

And so went the routine, day after day.

Early each morning Vahi-roa studied the sea against the background of fading stars. He set course by the sun and ocean swells. He adjusted constantly for wind and current. At sunset Vahi-roa waited for the stars to appear. Each night the home stars dropped lower in the sky behind.

Teva could not call the winds by name as did his grandfather, and he saw only two great ocean swells where Vahi-roa saw five. But in the silence of watching for signs, Teva learned something new each day. When he was alone with his thoughts, he longed for his mother, for the games of children, for the sights and sounds of his village. He often sang with the others of all they had left behind. They must never forget.

On the eighth night, as he had done on each of the previous seven, Vahi-roa tied another knot in the rope and said, "No longer do we look to the stars of our home waters."

Teva put down the line he was braiding. "What signs will you read now, Grandfather?"

Vahi-roa looked at the sky ahead. "See that reddish star? Its name is Star-Like-a-Father. The chants say it holds up the heavens above our destination."

Heeding his grandfather's directions, Teva found the star rising out of its pit in the east. Like all stars, it would arc into the sky, reach a high point, then set in the opposite pit. Each night it would rise higher.

Grandfather and grandson watched the star begin its climb. Vahi-roa then pointed up and said, "When Star-Like-a-Father passes above us, land will be near." He murmured a command to the steersman, and the canoe again shifted course.

Vahi-roa showed Teva two other stars marking islands that lay along the way. He told Teva the names spoken in the chants. Teva wiped the spray from his eyes and concentrated on the sky. All around him was a confusion of signs.

The moon rose, and Teva thought of his mother's story of a beautiful goddess who climbed into the sky to escape the burdens of earth. Perhaps tonight his mother looked at the same moon.

On the afternoon when the counting rope held fourteen knots, the canoe sailed into a squall. A sudden gust tossed white water over the hulls and swept a drenching rain across the decks. Laughing at raindrops that pelted them like small stones, a group of men and women trapped fresh water in one of the sails.

But as the canoe passed through the curtain of rain, a hush fell over everyone. The wind died. The air grew heavy. Sea and sky faded to gray. A crushing stillness fell upon them.

Vahi-roa looked around and saw a line of ripples moving toward the canoe. "We enter a new sea," he whispered. Teva felt the air stir for a moment, as if an invisible hand were passing before his face. Then all was still, except the lapping water beneath the hulls. *Ari'i* sat motionless in a silent sea.

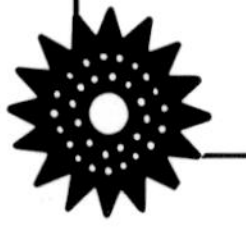

For days the voyagers waited beneath a burning sun. Sometimes a small breeze teased them, but soon it would die. Atop the sails, the pennants hung lifeless.

Each morning Vahi-roa searched the horizon for a sign of wind, but there was none. Each evening he tried to compare the position of the setting sun to the position of the first stars, but clouds hid the sky.

The women prayed for wind. The men chanted of the favorable winds of their home seas. Still the canoe drifted, and the heat wrapped it like a shroud.

Vahi-roa began to ration water and food. Because the canoe was not moving, the fishing lines hung empty. Like the others on board, Teva was thirsty and hungry. His blistered shoulders ached.

One morning Teva asked, "Are we lost, Grandfather?"

For several days Vahi-roa had taken only short naps. He rubbed his bloodshot eyes. "Quiet your doubts, Teva. The signs are there, but we are helpless without wind. We await what the gods bring us."

Teva looked at this strange new sea that challenged them. He vowed to keep his fears to himself.

On the night when the rope held twenty-two knots, something woke Teva from a dream. He sat up and felt something different. The canoe was moving! A new wind, cool and steady, carried *Ari'i-ati-tai* beneath a dome of stars. Teva joined his

grandfather on the platform.

Before Teva could speak, Vahi-roa pointed to the sky ahead of the canoe. "Look, Teva. A new star."

Teva found the star above the horizon, where it had hidden for many nights behind thick clouds.

Vahi-roa said, "The chants call it Star-That-Moves-in-One-Place."

Teva watched the star for a long time. Indeed, nearby stars rose and set in small arcs. This star moved in small circles and did not fall into a pit. Clouds might cover it, but when the clouds parted the star was still there. What did this mean?

As if reading his grandson's thoughts, Vahi-roa said, "We are more than half-way to our destination."

Teva looked up and found the reddish star. "It is as you said in the beginning, Grandfather. Star-Like-a-Father is passing almost overhead."

On the day when the rope held twenty-six knots, Vahi-roa watched a storm approach. The wind blew stronger and colder. Waves towered above the masts, then rolled beneath the canoe. Teva wore a grass cape over his shoulders and wrapped himself in a woven mat. The stinging spray still pierced him to the bone.

Then the storm struck.

Angry black clouds stole the daylight. Monster swells hid the horizon. As the winds grew in strength, men and women secured everything that moved and stripped and stowed the masts.

Above the screaming wind, Vahi-roa cried out, "Let the storm carry the canoe!"

The voyagers were in the hands of the gods. There was nothing to do but bail. Bail for their lives.

Darker grew the sky and stronger the storm's fury. A driving rain blinded them, and the sea threatened to swallow them. Teva clung to the deck and braced himself against the howling wind. Would *Ari'i* be buried in the sea like his father's canoe? Surely this canoe, blessed at each stage of its building, could not fail. Surely, *Ari'i* would ride out this storm.

Suddenly a huge wave crashed over the hulls. To Teva's horror, it swept one of the men into the sea. In a moment he was gone.

From his platform, Vahi-roa signaled for Teva to take the crewman's place.

Teva edged into the hull. A woman thrust a bailer into his hands. Teva bent to his task and tried not to think about the crewman swallowed by the sea.

What a struggle it was! *Ari'i* climbed each mountainous wave, hung at the top for a dizzying moment, then rushed down the other side only to face another wall of water. The storm raged into the night.

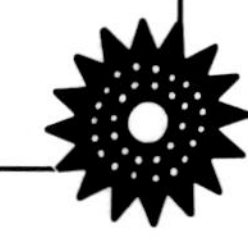

But *Ari'i-ati-tai* did not fail.

Finally the wind dropped. The rain lessened. Teva lay his head on his arms and fell asleep.

The boy awoke in the pale light of dawn. Someone had covered him with a mat. He felt the movement of the canoe. Was he dreaming? The masts were up! Once again the wind filled the sails.

Vahi-roa calmly read the weather and swells for the day. The wind was steady and strong, and the sun on the horizon gave him a solid steering sign. Three men held the center steering paddle, for the seas were still heavy. Some of the crew replaced torn lashings and repaired the sleeping hut. Others fed the animals and checked the provisions the storm had spared.

They had survived.

Later, their work done, the voyagers mourned the crewman lost to the storm.

Farewell, brave soul, farewell,
This new sea has claimed you.
For you, the way too long,
For you, the storm too strong,
Let the gods hear you,
Let the gods receive you,
Farewell, brave soul, farewell.

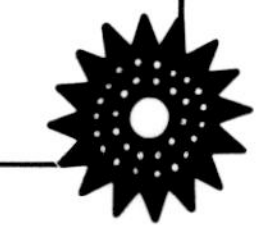

Teva knew that his grandfather must now locate the islands that would be their new home. It seemed an impossible task. The huge swells of this northern sea dwarfed the canoe. "How far has the storm blown us?" he asked.

Vahi-roa shook his head. "I am not sure. We must search for signs. The ocean is vast and an island is small." He patted the boy's shoulder.

"I know, Grandfather."

Vahi-roa steered a course upwind. The days passed slowly. The voyagers caught fresh fish and gratefully ate their fill. Still there were no signs of land.

In the evening when the counting rope held thirty-two knots, Vahi-roa still held to his course. The voyagers were blessed with clear skies. Teva scanned the heavens. Behind him their home star, Festivity-of-Chiefs, no longer rose to its old height. But Star-Like-a-Father was passing almost overhead.

Vahi-roa asked his grandson, "How high is Star-That-Moves-in-One-Place?"

Teva measured its height as he had been taught. "Two hands above the horizon, Grandfather."

"Good," said Vahi-roa. "It shines from a higher place."

"Another day without birds," said Teva. All day he had searched the skies for land birds that flew out to sea in the morning and returned to roost at dusk.

"Perhaps the land lies too far yet for birds," said Vahi-roa. "But land is there. Look and feel. *Ari'i* moves differently in this water. Something large has changed the waves. Have faith."

Another day passed and no birds appeared.

Now everyone searched the sea and sky. They must find land soon! All looked to Vahi-roa. His calm spirit was like an anchor keeping their hopes from drifting away.

At sunrise when the counting rope held thirty-four knots, Vahi-roa steered by two stars fading in the first light of morning. Teva searched the sky. Purple clouds hugged the horizon and promised good winds. Would today be another day of waiting? There was no food, not even taro gone sour.

Teva tried not to think of how empty his stomach felt. Others suffered far more than he.

All day the voyagers looked for signs of land—birds, the shape and color of clouds, drifting seaweed. They tasted the spray, and felt the temperature of the sea.

Then in the late afternoon, Teva saw them. Birds! High-flying birds. "They are returning to land, Grandfather!" he cried. Vahi-roa observed their direction and shifted course.

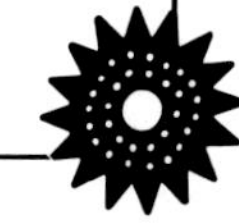

How restless everyone grew! They stared at the horizon and whispered among themselves. The animals fretted and whined in their cramped cages.

Day faded into evening. Stars appeared in the spaces between long lines of clouds. But there was no land.

While others slept fitfully, Vahi-roa stood on his platform, gazing at the stars. Teva stood with him, too excited to sleep. Side by side they waited for morning.

The next day dawned clear and cold. Teva checked the fishing lines. They were empty. Men and women huddled beneath soggy mats. Teva sipped some water from a gourd and wiped the encrusted salt from his eyelids. He must be vigilant.

The hours passed slowly. The sun sank lower in the sky.

Beneath the sinking sun, thick clouds clung to the horizon. They did not move like clouds driven by the wind.

Vahi-roa studied the clouds. "They wait for the sun," he said.

He spoke to the steersman, who adjusted the course. *Ari'i* sailed straight toward the bank of clouds and the setting sun.

Lower dropped the sun, and the clouds did not move. Now everyone watched. They spoke in hushed voices at this sunset unlike any other they had seen on their long voyage. Teva stood by his grandfather. Vahi-roa had read something in the clouds.

And then light burst from the clouds, and they saw what Vahi-roa had known from the chants. A great mountain! A mountain lit by the sun behind it! A mountain crowning an island!

Voices cried out in joy and thanksgiving. Men and women embraced and wept. Their laughter soared on the wind like the songs of birds.

Through his tears, Teva looked up at his grandfather. How strong the way-finder, how sure his knowledge. One day, he, Teva, would know his grandfather's sky. One day he, too, would find the way!

We followed the sea path north,
We sped on the trail of winds.
And now we approach your shores,
O Child of Tahiti!
A new sky above us,
A new sea around us,
A new land before us,
We offer our thanks,
And ask haven of thee.

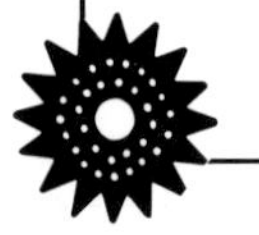

Publishers' Acknowledgment

We acknowledge the contributions of the many people who have assisted the author, the illustrator, and the publishers in creating this book: Myron B. Thompson, chair, steering committee, The *Hōkūle'a* Project; Marion Kelly, associate professor, Ethnic Studies Program, University of Hawaii; Will Kyselka, lecturer, Bishop Museum Planetarium; David B. K. Lyman, harbor pilot, Honolulu Harbor; Robert L. Pyle, curatorial assistant for birds, Bishop Museum; Yosihiko H. Sinoto, senior anthropologist, Bishop Museum; and Nainoa Thompson, navigator of the Polynesian sailing canoe, *Hōkūle'a*.

We also acknowledge the assistance of Gail Evenari Armstrong, Edith Kleinjans, Lee Kyselka, Shiho Nunes, Laura Thompson, and Eileen Tamura.

This book is a part of the *Hōkūle'a* Project, directed by Linda Menton at the Curriculum Research & Development Group of the University of Hawaii. The project is dedicated to sharing the knowledge of Polynesia's wayfinders, past and present, with children everywhere.